Our Emotions and Behavior

I Want to Win!

Sue Graves

**Illustrated by Emanuela Carletti
and Desideria Guicciardini**

free spirit
PUBLISHING®

During summer vacation, Bella went to Fun Club. Matt and Nell were the club leaders. They always thought of exciting things for everyone to do.

1

There were board games and floor games.
There were quizzes and puzzles.

There were things to make and bake and paint.

3

Bella always wanted to be **the best.**
She wanted to win everything.

If she didn't win, she **got mad.**

Matt said winning wasn't important.
He said it was important to **try hard**
and to be a **good sport**.

But Bella didn't listen.
She didn't want to be a good sport—ever!

One day, Matt and Nell had a **big surprise**.
They said everyone was going to make a tent. The best tent would win a prize.

Everyone made a tent. Most of the children tried their best. But Bella said it was too hard to make a tent.

Bella stopped trying. She got mad and **gave up**. Nell went to talk to her.

11

Nell said everyone finds some things hard to do. She said she couldn't ride a bike when she was little. She kept wobbling and falling off. But she didn't give up. She **kept trying**. Soon she could ride really well.

Bella thought about this. She said she would **try hard** to make a tent. She said she wouldn't give up until it was finished.

15

Bella did her best to make the tent.

She tried again . . .

. . . and again . . .

. . . and again.

At last the tent was finished. It looked a bit odd, but Bella was **proud** of herself anyway. She was pleased she had finished it.

17

Then everyone voted for the best tent.
Matt counted all the votes.

Everyone voted for Charlie's tent.
It was awesome!
Bella **felt happy** for Charlie.

Then Matt told everyone that he had another prize. This prize was for the person who had **tried the hardest**. He said that **Bella** had tried the hardest, and that she was a good sport, too.

Bella said being **a good sport**
was much nicer than getting mad.
She said it was more fun, too.

Everyone agreed!

Can you tell the story of what happens when the class has a competition to grow the tallest sunflower?

How do you think Billy felt when his sunflower didn't win? How did he feel when the children used all their flowers to make a display?

23

A note about sharing this book

The **Our Emotions and Behavior** series has been developed to provide a starting point for further discussion about children's feelings and behavior, in relation both to themselves and to other people.

I Want to Win!
This story looks at the importance of trying hard and being a good sport. It examines the problems that can arise when people find it hard to cope with disappointment or when they find it difficult to achieve ambitions. It looks at ways to overcome difficulties—and reminds us never to give up!

Picture story
The picture story on pages 22 and 23 provides an opportunity for speaking and listening. Children are encouraged to tell the story illustrated in the panels: The classmates are excited about the competition to grow the tallest sunflower. They each plant some seeds. They each water their plants carefully. Billy's sunflower, however, does not grow as tall as the other children's. He is getting more and more frustrated, and he is angry when he doesn't win. Then he sees all the sunflowers making a display and is pleased he made the effort to grow one after all.

How to use the book
The book is designed for adults to share with either an individual child or a group of children, and as a starting point for discussion.

The book also provides visual support and repeated words and phrases to build confidence in children who are starting to read on their own.

Before reading the story
Choose a time to read when you and the child are relaxed and have time to share the story.

Spend time looking at the illustrations and talk about what the book may be about before reading it together.

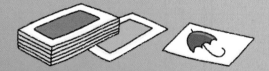

After reading, talk about the book with the children

- What was the story about? Have the children ever felt angry or upset because they have not won something or because they found something hard to do?

- Have they ever given up if something proved too difficult to do? What things do they find hard? Does everyone find the same things hard or do different people find different things difficult?

- Ask the children to recall instances when they tried hard to achieve something. How did they feel if they succeeded? How did they feel if they tried hard and did not succeed? Conversely, how did they feel if they gave up without really trying?

- Ask the children why they think it is important to be a good sport. Ask them to recount events from their own experiences when they had to be good sports about something.

- Suggest that children draw "before" and "after" pictures of times when they have found something difficult in the past. In the "before" picture, ask them to draw themselves and the challenge they were frustrated or intimidated by. In the "after" picture, ask them to draw themselves staying calm, persevering, and overcoming the challenge.

To Isabelle, William A., George, William G., Max, Emily, Leo, Caspar, Felix, and Phoebe—S.G.

Published in North America by Free Spirit Publishing Inc., Minneapolis, Minnesota, 2017

Library of Congress Cataloging-in-Publication Data
Names: Graves, Sue, 1950– author. | Carletti, Emanuela, illustrator. | Guicciardini, Desideria, illustrator.
Title: I want to win! / written by Sue Graves ; illustrated by Emanuela Carletti and Desideria Guicciardini.
Description: Minneapolis : Free Spirit Publishing, [2017] | Series: Our emotions and behavior
Identifiers: LCCN 2016032258| ISBN 9781631981319 (hardcover) | ISBN 1631981315 (hardcover)
Subjects: LCSH: Performance in children—Juvenile literature. | Failure (Psychology) in children—Juvenile literature. | Success in children—Juvenile literature. | Perseverance (Ethics)—Juvenile literature. | Sportsmanship—Juvenile literature.
Classification: LCC BF723.P365 G73 2017 | DDC 155.4—dc23
LC record available at https://lccn.loc.gov/2016032258

Reading Level Grade 1; Interest Level Ages 4–8 ; Fountas & Pinnell Guided Reading Level I

10 9 8 7 6 5 4 3 2 1
Printed in China
S14101016

Free Spirit Publishing Inc.
6325 Sandburg Road, Suite 100
Minneapolis, MN 55427-3674
(612) 338-2068
help4kids@freespirit.com
www.freespirit.com

First published in 2017 by Franklin Watts, a division of Hachette Children's Books • London, UK, and Sydney, Australia

Text © Franklin Watts 2017
Illustrations © Emanuela Carletti and Desideria Guicciardini 2017

The rights of Sue Graves to be identified as the author and Emanuela Carletti and Desideria Guicciardini as the illustrators of this Work have been asserted in accordance with the Copyright, Designs and Patents Act, 1988.

Editor: Jackie Hamley
Designer: Peter Scoulding